For: C.C., J.B., S.A.F. and everyone rebuilding

DIAL BOOKS FOR YOUNG READERS

Penguin Young Readers Group

An imprint of Penguin Random House LLC

375 Hudson Street

New York, New York 10014

Copyright © 2018 by Cori Doerrfeld

ISBN 9780735229358

Printed in China

20

Design by Jennifer Kelly

Text set in Poliphilus MT Std

The artwork for this book was created with digital ink and a whole lotta heart.

THE RABBIT
LISTENED

BY

CORI
DOERRFELD

 DIAL BOOKS FOR YOUNG READERS

One day, Taylor decided to build something.

Something new.

Something special.

Something amazing.

Taylor was so proud.

But then, out of nowhere . . .

things came crashing down.

The chicken was the first to notice.

"Cluck, cluck! What a shame!
I'm so sorry, sorry, sorry this happened!"

"Let's talk, talk,
talk about it!
Cluck, cluck!"

But Taylor didn't feel like talking.

So the chicken left.

Next came the bear.

"Grarr! Rarr! How horrible! I bet you feel so angry!
Let's shout about it! Garrr! RARRR! GRAAAAR!"

But Taylor didn't
feel like shouting.

So the bear left.

The elephant knew just what to do.

"Trumpa-da! I can fix this!
We just need to remember *exactly*
the way things were."

But Taylor didn't feel
like remembering.

So the elephant also left.

One by one, they came.

The hyena: "Hee-hee!
Let's laugh about it!"

The ostrich: "Gulp!
Let's hide and pretend
nothing happened!"

The kangaroo: "Tsk tsk.
What a mess! Let's throw
it all away!"

And the snake: "Shhhhh.
Let'ssss go knock down
someone else'ssss."

But Taylor didn't feel like doing
anything with anybody.

So eventually, they all left . . .

until Taylor was alone.

In the quiet, Taylor didn't
even notice the rabbit.

But it moved closer,
and closer.

Until Taylor could feel
its warm body.

Together they sat in silence
until Taylor said,
"Please stay with me."

The rabbit listened.

The rabbit listened as
Taylor talked.

The rabbit listened as
Taylor shouted.

The rabbit
listened as Taylor
remembered . . .

and laughed.

The rabbit listened to Taylor's
plans to hide . . .

to throw everything away . . .

to ruin things for someone else.

Through it all, the rabbit never left.

And when the time was right, the rabbit listened
to Taylor's plan to build again.

"I can't wait," Taylor said.

"It's going to be amazing."